A church is a weighty thing, isn't it? Its doors are heavy and hard to budge. Its walls are made of stone. The steps you climb to enter it can make your legs tired. If the ceiling is very high, you might feel very small.

And a church might have pictures of people or things that are scary.

Still, there are many good reasons to visit a church.

One reason is to look at the pictures to find out what the people who made them believed. And the pictures almost always tell stories.

My mother had a special way to visit a church—it was light, not scary, and even kind of floaty.

We called it

SAINT SPOTTING

SAINT SPOTTING

OR

HOW TO READ A CHURCH

CHRIS RASCHKA

EERDMANS BOOKS FOR YOUNG READERS
GRAND RAPIDS, MICHIGAN

Published in 2021 by
Eerdmans Books for Young Readers
an imprint of Wm. B. Eerdmans Publishing Co.
Grand Rapids, Michigan • www.eerdmans.com/youngreaders

 • Manufactured in China

29 28 27 26 25 24 23 22 21 1 2 3 4 5 6 7 8 9

A catalog record of this book is available
from the Library of Congress.

ISBN 978-0-8028-5521-3

Illustrations created with
watercolor.

FSC www.fsc.org MIX Paper from responsible sources FSC® C104723

FOR MY MOTHER

Here's how you do it.

Look at this map. It shows you all the saints we'll spot today.

1 St. ANTHONY
2 St. RITA
3 St. CATHERINE
4 St. AGNES
5 St. ANDREW
6 St. SEBASTIAN
7 St. BARTHOLOMEW
8 St. ZENO
9 St. FRANCIS
10 St. LUCY
11 St. CECILIA
12 St. NICHOLAS
13 St. PETER
14 St. PAUL
15 St. MATTHEW
16 St. MARK
17 St. LUKE
18 St. JOHN
19 St. MARY AND JESUS
20 St. ELIZABETH
21 St. MARY MAGDALENE
22 St. JOHN THE BAPTIST
23 JESUS CHRIST
24 St. JOSEPH
25 St. MARTHA
26 St. CHRISTOPHER
27 St. BARBARA
28 FAITH
29 HOPE
30 CHARITY
31 St. BRIDGET
32 St. JEROME
33 St. AUGUSTINE
34 St. EUSTACE
35 St. MONICA
36 St. ROSE OF LIMA
37 St. MARGARET
38 St. GEORGE

20
21
19
22
14
24
25
13
23
15
26
16
18
17
27
12
11
10
9
8
28
7
29
30
6
5
4
31
32
3
33
34
35
2
38
37
36
1

Saints are people who are important in the history of the Christian faith.

They always have stories of their own which give you clues to recognize them.

For instance, Saint Anthony was kind and loved reading, so you will see him holding a book or a baby (usually Jesus as a baby) or both.

And Saint Rita had a wound which never healed. She is the saint of suffering. Sometimes people think of her when something has been bothering them for a long time too.

SAINT CATHERINE

When saints are killed for what they believe, they are called martyrs.

Here is Saint Catherine with her wheel, which was made to kill her as punishment for teaching the emperor's wife about Jesus. When the wheel failed, poor Saint Catherine was killed with a sword.

The symbol for Saint Agnes is a lamb.

Both of these saints were killed because they refused to marry the rich men who desired them. They wanted to live simply, as nuns.

Nuns study, serve, and pray.

Sometimes a saint's symbol has something to do with how they were martyred, but not always.

Here are four saints and their symbols:
Saint Andrew—an X-shaped cross.
Saint Sebastian—arrows.
Saint Bartholomew—his own skin.
Saint Zeno—a fishing pole.

Saint Zeno might or might not have been martyred (it's a complicated story) but he certainly wasn't martyred with a fishing pole.
He just liked to fish!

Saint Sebastian was always my favorite because he's easy to spot.

More saints and symbols:

Saint Nicholas's symbol is three bags of gold, which he gave to the poor. Our story of Santa Claus comes from him.

Saint Cecilia–musical instruments.

Saint Lucy–her eyes. She is the saint of vision. (Pictures of Saint Lucy always terrified me.)

Saint Francis is the saint of animals. He preached to the birds and called them his little brothers and sisters, which made people think he was crazy (but which is true if you think about it the way Saint Francis did).

SAINT NICHOLAS

SAINT CECILIA

SAINT LUCY

SAINT FRANCIS

SAiNT PeteR

Saint Peter carries
a key, which is the key
to heaven that Jesus gave him.
It could also mean knowledge and
understanding.

Saint Paul carries a book to show us
his great wisdom and learning. He
also might have a sword, not because
he was a soldier but because that
was how he was killed.

SAINT MATTHEW
SAINT JOHN

Here are
four saints–
the Evangelists–
who usually go together.
The Evangelists wrote the
four main stories of Jesus,
which, all together, are called
the Gospels.

Each saint has symbols:
Matthew–a man.
Mark–a lion.
Luke–an ox.
John–an eagle, a goblet,
and a snake.

These four saints
are often found
near each other
in a church.

Now we're coming to the front of the church.

Here is Saint Mary, the mother of Jesus. She is also called the Holy Mother, the Madonna, or the Blessed Virgin Mary. You usually see her holding the baby Jesus in her lap, so she's easy to find.

Saint Elizabeth was
Mary's cousin
and the mother
of Saint John
the Baptist.
Saint Elizabeth
thought she was
too old to have a
baby (she was much
older than Mary)
but John was born
in spite of her
doubts.

Saint Mary Magdalene was a friend and follower of Jesus. Her symbols are long hair and a jar of ointment.

Saint John the Baptist told everyone that Jesus was coming. Saint John the Baptist's symbols are a long-stemmed cross, a fur cloak, a honey pot or hive (because he lived in the wilderness), and a lamb (which itself represents Jesus).

Jesus is the reason for
churches being around at all.
People who believe in the stories
and teachings of Jesus are called
Christians, and churches are
their holy places.

And here at last is Jesus. Jesus is also called Jesus Christ. Christ is a Greek word meaning Messiah, or chosen one. Jesus is always found at the most holy spot in a church: above or behind the altar.

Christians believe Jesus was a living person, like all people, but also divine, because he is the Son of God. Jesus is often shown on a cross, just before his death. This is meant to emphasize his real life and death. When he looks down, we know that he cares for all in life who suffer. His symbols are a cross, a fish, or a lamb.

SAINT JOSEPH

Saint Joseph was the earthly father of Jesus. He is remembered for poverty, chastity, and obedience. His symbols are carpenter's tools.

Saint Martha was another friend of Jesus. Her symbol is a ladle, because she loved to serve.

Sometimes a church may give you stories, like these two, that are not found in the Bible.

In his legend, Saint Christopher carried the baby Jesus across a river, and Jesus grew into a man as they went.

Saint Christopher's symbols are the baby Jesus and a staff.

Saint Barbara was shut into a tower by her father. Alone, she studied the sky and the stars and came to believe in the teachings of Jesus.

Her symbol is a tower.

These aren't saints really but ideas.

Faith–a cross.
Hope–an anchor.
Charity–a heart.

If you find yourself in a church with no saints, then you are probably in a Protestant church. Five hundred years ago, Protestant Christians protested against some of the doings of the Roman Catholic Church, which was the main church of Christians in the western world at that time. Among their protests was this: There are too many saints!

So that's how my mother and I visit a church. She likes the paintings and stories. I like the arrows.

Once, churches were called the Bibles of the Poor. Even if you didn't have a Bible (and no one besides priests and monks and nuns did back then), and even if you couldn't read, you could

learn all the important stories by studying the pictures you saw on the old churches' walls.

Saint Sebastian is still my favorite.